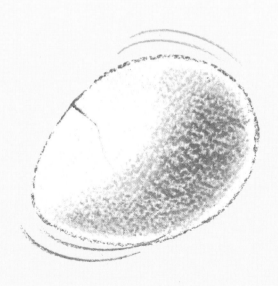

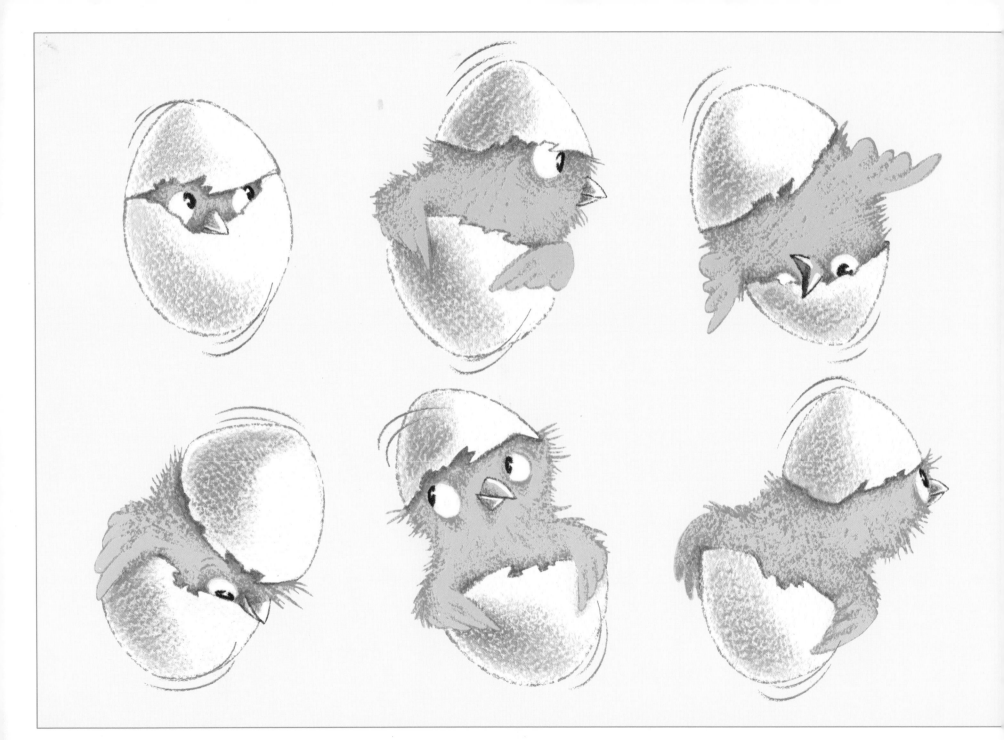

PIP & PUP

EUGENE YELCHIN

GODWINBOOKS

Henry Holt and Company

NEW YORK

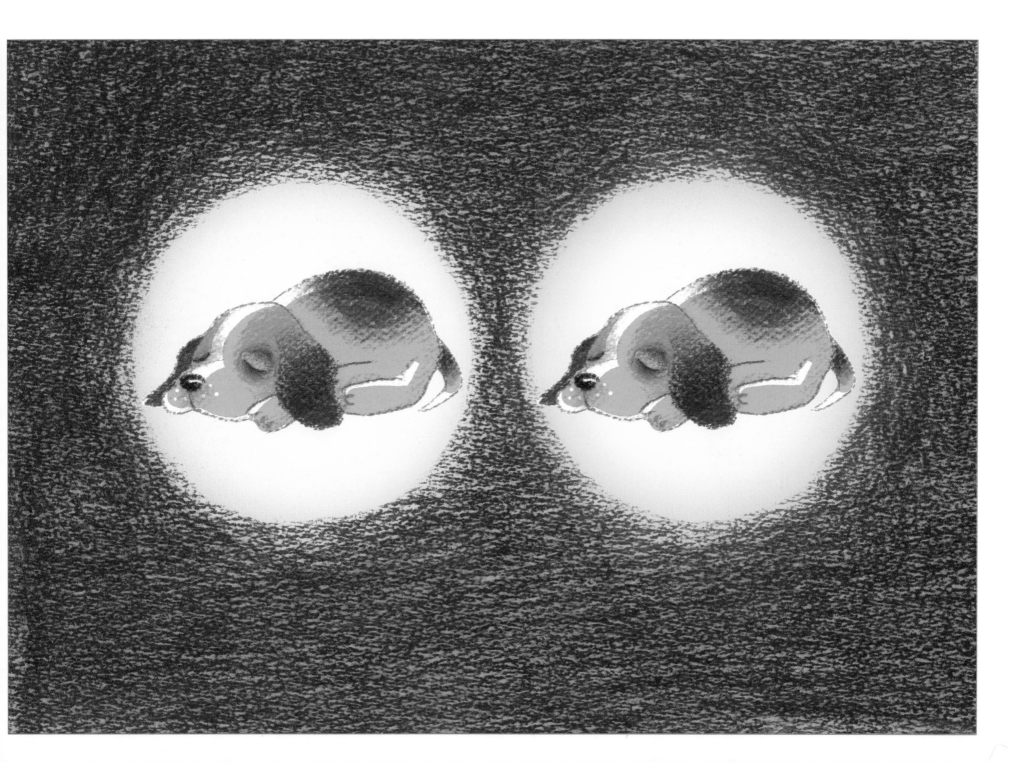

To Isaac and Ezra

Henry Holt and Company, *Publishers since 1866*
Henry Holt® is a registered trademark of Macmillan Publishing Group, LLC
175 Fifth Avenue, New York, NY 10010
mackids.com

Library of Congress Control Number: 2017932704
ISBN 978-1-62779-394-0

Our books may be purchased in bulk for promotional, educational, or business use. Please contact your local bookseller or the Macmillan
Corporate and Premium Sales Department at (800) 221-7945 ext. 5442 or by e-mail at MacmillanSpecialMarkets@macmillan.com.

First edition, 2018

The artist used colored pencils, oil pastels, and digital painting.
Printed in China by RR Donnelley Asia Printing Solutions Ltd., Dongguan City, Guangdong Province
1 3 5 7 9 10 8 6 4 2